COMIC CHAPTER BOOKS

™

STONE ARCH BOOKS
a capstone imprint

Published in 2016 by Stone Arch Books,
A Capstone Imprint
1710 Roe Crest Drive,
North Mankato, Minnesota 56003
www.mycapstone.com

Copyright © 2016 Hanna-Barbera.
SCOOBY-DOO and all related characters and elements
are trademarks of and © Hanna-Barbera.
WB SHIELD: ™ & © Warner Bros. Entertainment Inc.
(S16)

CAPS35806

All rights reserved. No part of this publication may be
reproduced in whole or in part, or stored in a retrieval
system, or transmitted in any form or by any means,
electronic, mechanical, photocopying, recording, or
otherwise, without written permission of the publisher.

Cataloging-in-Publication Data is available on the Library
of Congress website.

ISBN: 978-1-4965-3586-3 (library binding)
ISBN: 978-1-4965-3590-0 (paperback)
ISBN: 978-1-4965-3594-8 (eBook PDF)

Summary: While Scooby-Doo and the gang visit a
tourist town, the Mystery Machine vanishes in a patch
of thick fog. Other vehicles have gone missing as well.
Mystery Inc. is on the case! But can they unravel the
mystery of the Mist Monster, or will they get lost in
the fog?

Printed and bound in the USA.
009938R

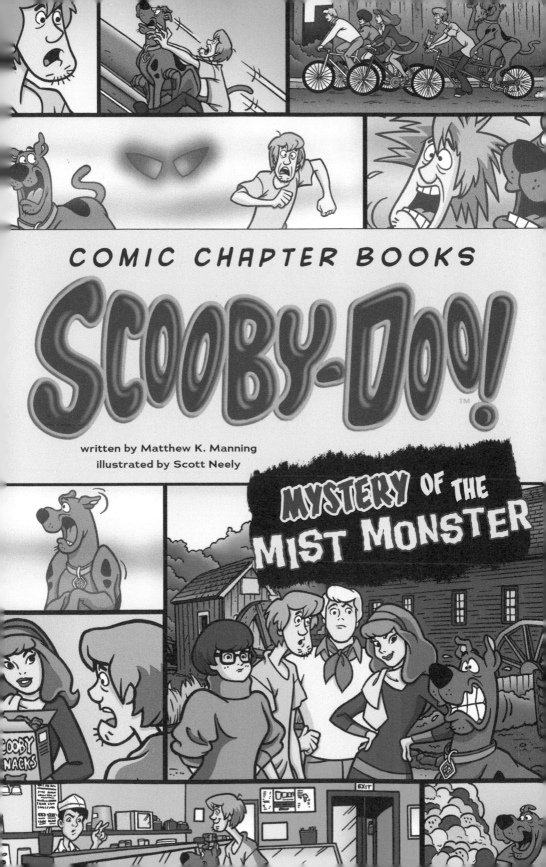

COMIC CHAPTER BOOKS

SCOOBY-DOO!

written by Matthew K. Manning
illustrated by Scott Neely

MYSTERY OF THE MIST MONSTER

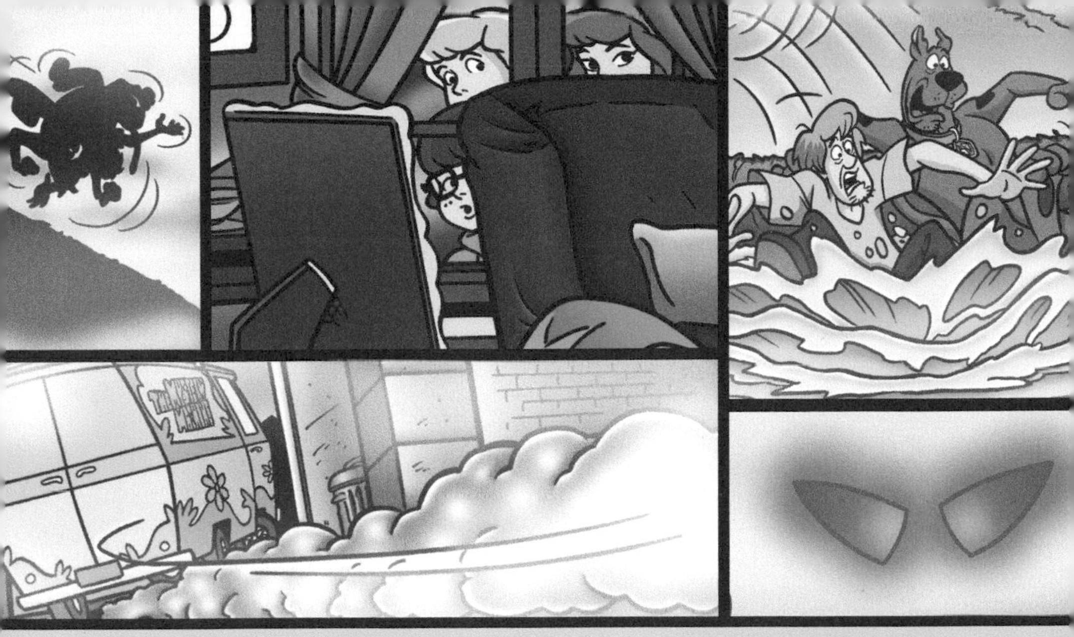

TABLE OF CONTENTS

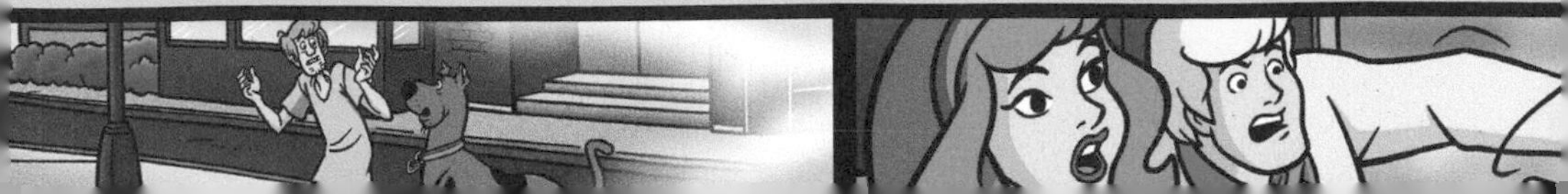

MEET MYSTERY INC.

SCOOBY-DOO

SKILLS: LOYAL; SUPER SNOUT
BIO: THIS HAPPY-GO-LUCKY HOUND
AVOIDS SCARY SITUATIONS AT ALL
COSTS, BUT HE'LL DO ANYTHING FOR
A SCOOBY SNACK!

SHAGGY ROGERS

SKILLS: LUCKY; HEALTHY APPETITE
BIO: THIS LAID-BACK DUDE WOULD RATHER LOOK FOR GRUB THAN SEARCH FOR CLUES, BUT HE USUALLY FINDS BOTH!

FRED JONES, JR.

SKILLS: ATHLETIC; CHARMING
BIO: THE LEADER AND OLDEST MEMBER OF THE GANG. HE'S A GOOD SPORT — AND GOOD AT THEM, TOO!

DAPHNE BLAKE

SKILLS: BRAINS; BEAUTY
BIO: AS A SIXTEEN-YEAR-OLD FASHION QUEEN, DAPHNE SOLVES HER MYSTERIES IN STYLE.

VELMA DINKLEY

SKILLS: CLEVER; HIGHLY INTELLIGENT
BIO: ALTHOUGH SHE'S THE YOUNGEST MEMBER OF MYSTERY INC., VELMA'S AN OLD PRO AT CATCHING CROOKS.

CHAPTER 1

VROOOOOOM!

The Mystery Machine's engine roared as the van sped down a winding road.

Fred had the van's high beams on, but it didn't seem to be making much of a difference. He hadn't been able to clearly see the road in front of him ever since they had exited the highway at Mystic, Connecticut.

"We should pull over," said Daphne. She was sitting next to him on the van's front seat.

"We're almost there," said Fred. He kept his eyes on the road as he spoke. "This mist came out of nowhere."

"Like, I'm with Daphne," came a voice from behind them. Shaggy was sitting on the floor in the back of the van, holding his stomach. "My tummy's been grumbling for a half hour. I say we park this thing and get some grub."

"Shaggy," said Fred, "we just ate lunch a half hour ago!"

"Isn't that what I just said?" Shaggy asked, puzzled. He looked over to Scooby-Doo, who sat next to him on the van's shag carpet. Scooby shrugged. He thought Shaggy had made himself perfectly clear.

"Turn right at the next street," Velma instructed as she studied a giant unfolded map of Connecticut. It was so big, Fred couldn't even see out of her side of the van. If the fog wasn't making it hard enough for him to drive, Velma certainly wasn't helping.

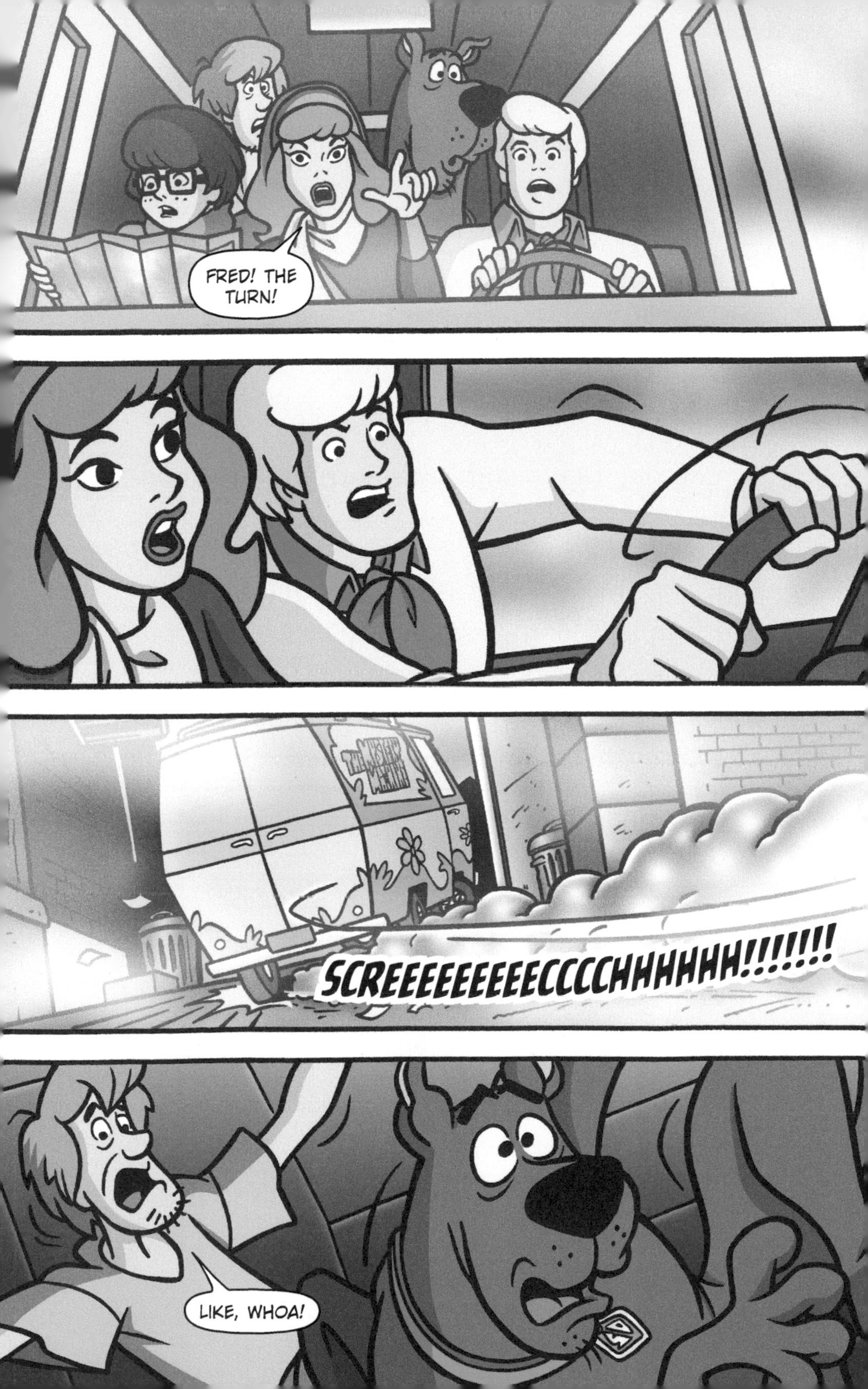
FRED! THE TURN!
SCREEEEEEEEEECCCCHHHHHH!!!!!!!
LIKE, WHOA!

As Fred made the sudden turn, Velma heard a loud bang in the back of the van.

WHUMP!

She turned to see what had happened. "You guys okay?" she asked the pile on the van floor that resembled Scooby and Shaggy.

Scooby-Doo held his stomach and groaned. "Rouch!" he barked.

"What's the matter, Scoobs?" Shaggy asked his canine friend. "Is anything broken, old pal?"

Scooby shook his head.

"Are you hurt?" Shaggy pressed.

Scooby shook his head again. "Rungry!" he told his friend.

GRUMMMMBLE Scooby-Doo's grumbling stomach echoed throughout the van.

"Good news, guys," said Fred. "We're here!"

"Great," said Shaggy, patting Scooby on the back. "Maybe you can get something to eat — and maybe I'll joined you." He smiled.

The van pulled down the alley and into a parking lot behind an old hotel. The Mystery Inc. gang filed out of the vehicle. Shaggy and Scooby stretched and then looked at each other. The fog was so thick, Shaggy could barely make out his faithful Great Dane.

"Scoob?" Shaggy said. "Are you there, old buddy?"

"Rover here," said Scooby-Doo. He waved his paws in front of Shaggy's face.

"Jinkies," said Velma as she walked over toward her friends. "You're not kidding around. This fog is as thick as soup."

"Soup?" said Shaggy. "Did someone say soup?"

"Ru-huh!" Scooby chimed in.

"Like, that's the best idea you've had today," said Shaggy. "Mystic is famous for its clam chowder, right? I say we take a lunch break."

"Your encore lunch will have to wait," said Fred. "Let's at least check in at the hotel first."

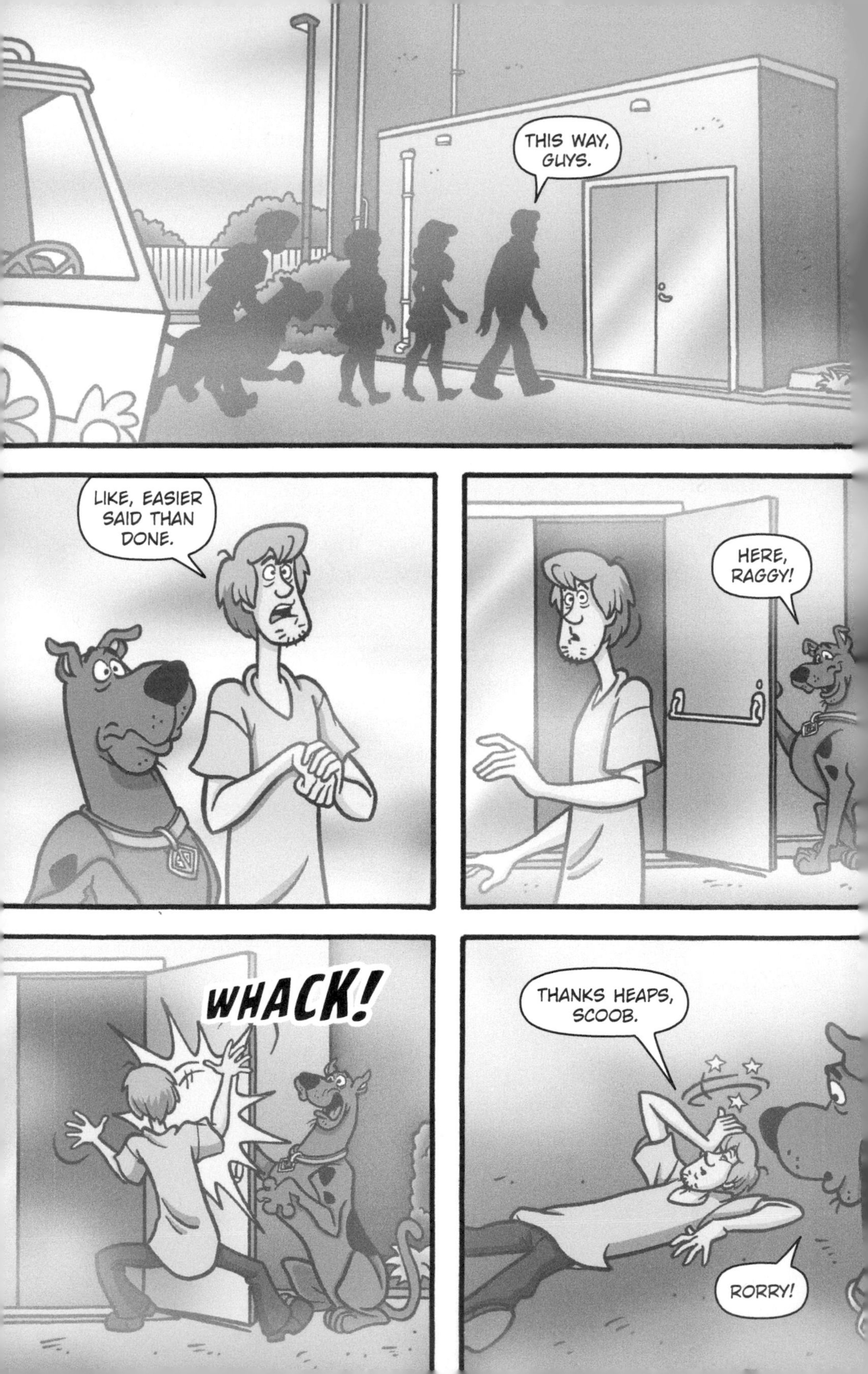
THIS WAY, GUYS.
LIKE, EASIER SAID THAN DONE.
HERE, RAGGY!
WHACK!
THANKS HEAPS, SCOOB.
RORRY!

Once inside, the gang walked down a dark hallway and into the hotel's lobby. The room was small and empty, except for a row of chairs by the front window. The window looked out onto Main Street. But at the moment, it just looked out onto a sea of fog.

Shaggy walked up to the desk and smacked the small bell with his palm.

BRRRING!

Nothing happened.

He looked back at Daphne, who was standing behind him. "Some service, huh?"

"Just be patient, Shaggy," she said.

"Tell that to my stomach," he said, as he turned back around. "Zoinks!" The concierge was standing behind the desk all of the sudden.

"May I help you?" the thin man muttered.

"L-like, we have a reservation?" Shaggy replied. It came out more like a question.

"Of course," the concierge said. He typed something into the computer in front of him.

His dark eyes seemed to be at war with their heavy eyelids. It was almost like his guests were putting him to sleep. "Name?" he said after an awkward silence.

"It's under Daphne Blake," Daphne said, taking a step toward the desk. "So what's there to do around here that's fun?"

The man behind the desk didn't answer. He just continued to type at his computer. He then handed Daphne a key and a small piece of paper.

"You're room 4912," he said. "Please put this parking pass on your windshield to avoid having your van towed after business hours."

Fred took the ticket from Daphne. He nodded at the concierge and then headed down the hallway toward the back entrance. "I'll get the bags," Fred said.

"We'll help," said Shaggy, following along.

"Thanks, guys," said Fred.

"Anything to get us to the restaurant quicker!" Shaggy exclaimed.

Fred rolled his eyes as he pushed open the back door. "Hey, the fog has cleared," he said.

"Like, that's not all," Shaggy said. "So has the Mystery Machine!"

There were three cars parked in the now visible parking lot. None were the blue van.

"So, like, where do we put the parking pass?" Shaggy wondered.

But Fred wasn't listening. He was running back inside the hotel.

Scooby and Shaggy looked at each other, shrugged, and then followed their friend. Shaggy's stomach was still rumbling, but he hardly noticed it now.

CHAPTER 2
MONSTER IN THE MIST

"This doesn't make any sense," said Daphne. "It was right here."

The entire Mystery Inc. gang was standing in the parking lot, looking around.

"Someone stole it," said Velma. "It's the only explanation."

"What if it was towed?" Fred suggested.

"Unlikely," said Velma. "The concierge said that cars weren't towed until after business hours. It's only one in the afternoon."

"It'd be a lot easier to steal a car in a thick fog," said Daphne.

She was looking away from the parking lot now, toward Mystic River. The river was visible behind a row of condos that lined a dock. And past the river was the thick fog. It appeared to have drifted to the opposite shore.

"Hmm," said Fred. "Might be worth checking out."

"It can't hurt," said Velma.

GRUMMMMBLE

"Row!" Scooby-Doo groaned, clutching his hungry stomach again.

"It could hurt a little," Shaggy suggested. "Scoobs needs something to eat — like, lickety-split!"

"Reah," said Scooby-Doo. "A ranana split!"

"I don't have a banana split," Velma replied, "but I do have some Scooby Snacks." She shook a boxful of Scooby's favorite treats. Velma pulled one out and tossed it to Scooby.

GULP!

"Rummy!" Scooby exclaimed, swallowing the tasty treat.

Fred, Daphne, and Velma didn't waste any time. They started jogging down the alley toward Main Street.

"It's never a good sign when they start running," Shaggy said as he looked over at his dog. "Like, we should think for ourselves for once and run in the other direction."

Scooby nodded in agreement.

Shaggy sighed. "Oh well," he said. "Why start now?" Then he and Scooby revved up their legs and took off after their friends.

They followed the gang onto Main Street, and then over the drawbridge that connected one side of the river to the other. But by the time they got to the opposite side of the bridge, the gang was forced to slow down. The fog was so thick, it was their only option. They could barely see three steps ahead of themselves.

"This fog is almost unnatural," Velma said.

"I'd say it's supernatural," suggested Shaggy. He and Scooby exchanged a look and then a shiver.

"It is strange," Daphne added. "I'll give it that. I've never seen anything like —"

But Daphne didn't finish her sentence. Instead, she froze in her tracks. It was like she was suddenly unable to move. She just stared ahead down Main Street, her eyes widened and her mouth dropped slightly open.

Fred looked at her, and then strained to see what she was staring at. "What's the matter?" he asked.

Daphne didn't answer. There wasn't a need to. Because coming toward the gang were two glowing red eyes. They seemed to be floating through the fog. Whatever creature they belonged to was enormous and seemed to be making some sort of noise.

The creature sounded like it was humming.

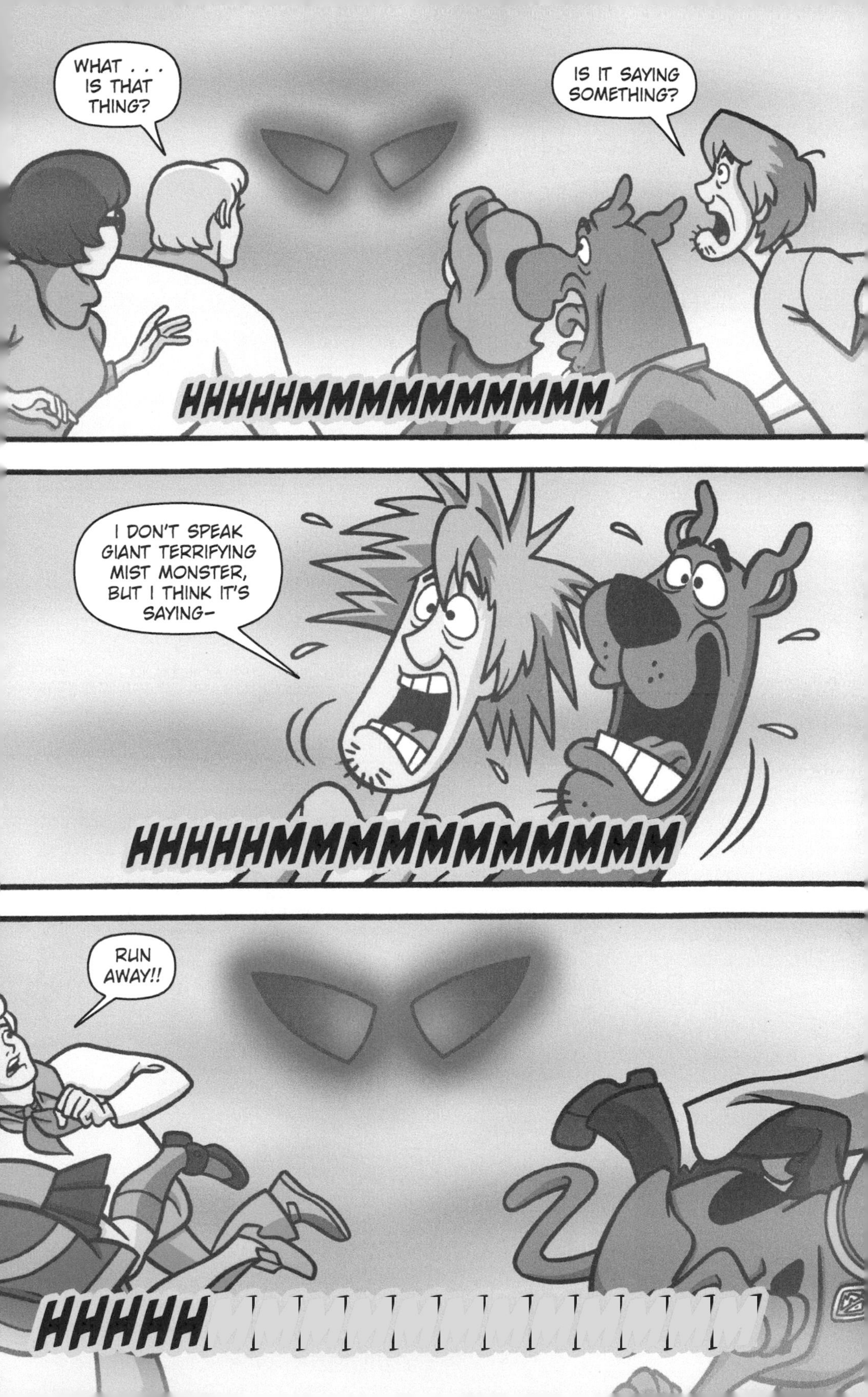
WHAT . . . IS THAT THING?
IS IT SAYING SOMETHING?
HHHHHMMMMMMMMMMMM
I DON'T SPEAK GIANT TERRIFYING MIST MONSTER, BUT I THINK IT'S SAYING–
HHHHHMMMMMMMMMMMMM
RUN AWAY!!
HHHHH

"Lock the door!" Shaggy yelled as they dashed into the hotel. "Board the windows! Stockpile milk and bread! Everybody panic!"

Fred stood in front of the window. He looked out in the direction of the bridge. "I don't think that'll be necessary, Shaggy," he said. "It's not following us."

"Looks like the fog is completely gone, too!" said Daphne.

"And it took the Mist Monster with it," said Velma as she collapsed onto one of the lobby's chairs, completely out of breath.

"Well that's a relief," said Shaggy. He sat down next to Velma. "Let's all just pile back in the Mystery Machine and get out of this crazy one-monster town."

"There's only one problem with that plan," said Velma.

"Ro ran," said Scooby.

"Yep," said Velma. "No van. The Mystery Machine is still missing. And all our luggage is with it."

"Oh no!" Shaggy said, suddenly standing up in a hurry.

"What?" asked Daphne.

"It's worse than we thought! It's worse than anything we could have ever imagined!" he exclaimed. He was pacing back and forth in the lobby now. He trembled in fear.

"Calm down and tell us what's wrong," said Daphne.

"It was in my bag, and now it's . . . now it's gone!" said Shaggy.

"What?" asked Velma. She was standing now, too.

"Our emergency snack stash!" said Shaggy.

Fred, Daphne, and Velma all shook their heads, and then sat back down in the lobby chairs. "Geez, Shaggy," said Fred. "We thought it was something serious."

Scooby and Shaggy exchanged a concerned look. "Like, can he just not hear me today?" Shaggy asked his friend.

"Ron't rask me," Scooby replied with a shrug.

SNIFF! SNIFF! SNIFF!

Scooby-Doo sniffed the air with his sensitive snout. He glanced around the lobby until he spotted the source of the sweet aroma.

"Rints!" said Scooby, pointing a paw at the concierge's desk.

Shaggy spotted two bowls of red and white striped candies on the desk. "Mints!" he repeated, licking his lips.

The two friends rushed toward the desk. "Oh no!" shouted the concierge, stopping them. "Only one per customer!"

"Like, perfect," said Shaggy.

"Reah," added Scooby-Doo. "Rerfect!"

The friends each picked up one bowl. Shaggy dumped the entire bowl into his mouth, and Scooby followed with his own bowl.

"Thanks!" said Shaggy.

"Rhanks!" Scooby repeated.

The concierge sighed.

Scooby-Doo and Shaggy both sat down next to their friends. That snack would tide them over for at least a few minutes.

CHAPTER 3
CIDER MILL THRILL

"Bicycles?" said Shaggy. It wasn't really a question. He'd heard what the concierge had said. He just didn't think he could be serious.

"Yes, bicycles," the concierge repeated.

"Sounds great," said Velma, standing at the hotel's front desk. She looked more excited than Shaggy thought she had any right to.

"The shop is two blocks past the bridge," said the concierge. "They have plenty to rent."

"Thanks so much," said Velma, before turning to face the rest of the gang. "C'mon!"

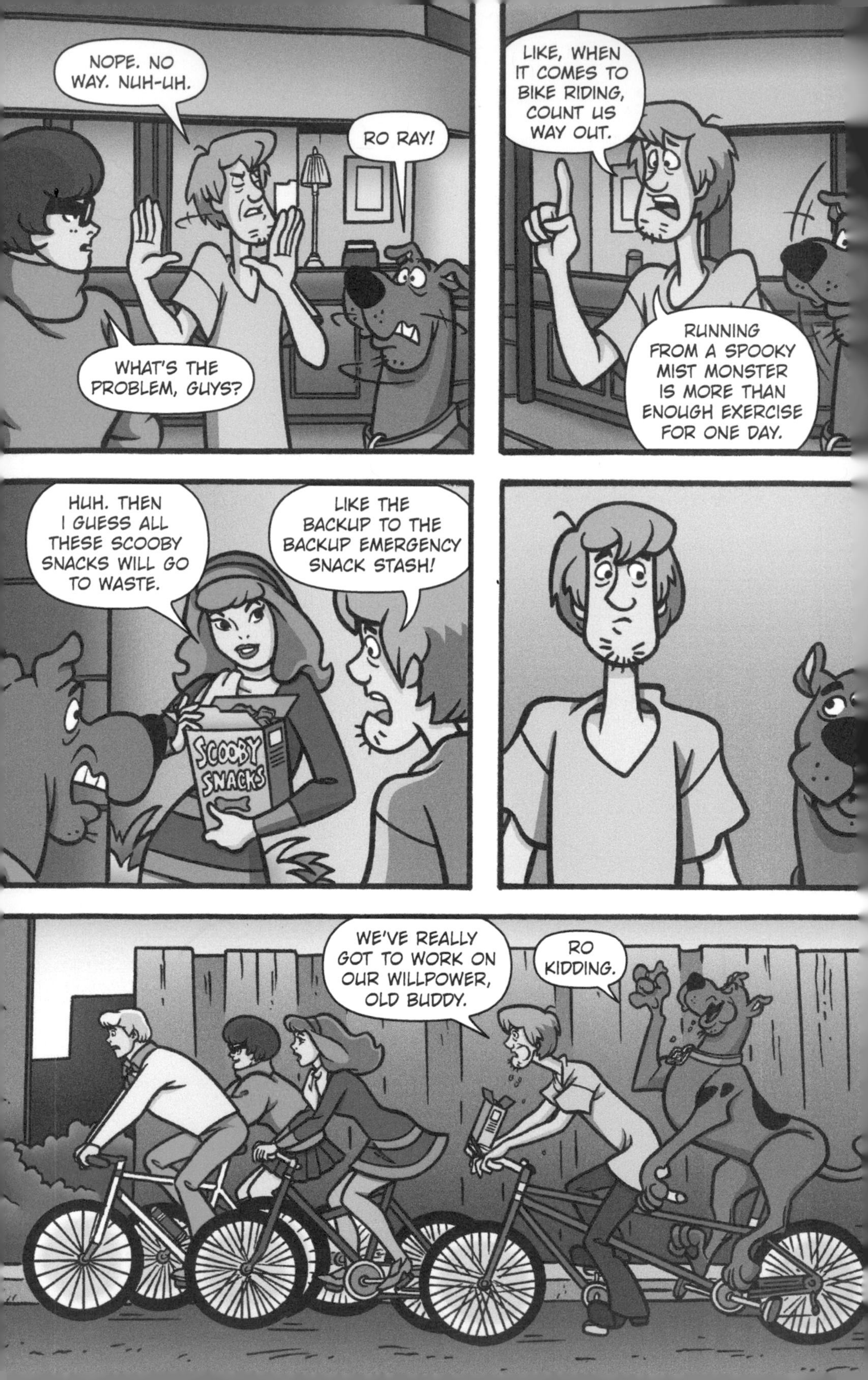
NOPE. NO WAY. NUH-UH.
RO RAY!
WHAT'S THE PROBLEM, GUYS?
LIKE, WHEN IT COMES TO BIKE RIDING, COUNT US WAY OUT.
RUNNING FROM A SPOOKY MIST MONSTER IS MORE THAN ENOUGH EXERCISE FOR ONE DAY.
HUH. THEN I GUESS ALL THESE SCOOBY SNACKS WILL GO TO WASTE.
LIKE THE BACKUP TO THE BACKUP EMERGENCY SNACK STASH!
SCOOBY SNACKS
WE'VE REALLY GOT TO WORK ON OUR WILLPOWER, OLD BUDDY.
RO KIDDING.

With their bikes rented, the gang set out to explore Mystic. The fog was completely gone. It made bike riding much easier than their earlier drive in the Mystery Machine.

"So what's the plan?" Daphne asked. She sped up a little to keep pace with Fred.

"Well, if we want to leave this town, we'll definitely need to find our van," he replied. "But I don't even know where to start looking."

"We need a place with locals," Velma said from behind the two. "Somewhere we can find out more about this so-called Mist Monster."

"Not a bad idea," said Fred. "But where?"

"I don't think we have a choice in the matter," said Daphne. Fred looked over to her, and then over his shoulder. Scooby and Shaggy were nowhere to be seen.

"Where did they —?" But Fred didn't need to finish his thought. He noticed a smell in the air. It was the smell of fresh apple cinnamon donuts. He turned his bike around, and Daphne and Velma followed.

A small cider mill stood on the side of the road. It was an old-fashioned sort of place. It looked like it had stopped being operational as an actual mill years ago and had become a tourist attraction of sorts. It was the kind of place that sold fresh apple cider, jams and jellies, and donuts.

"Guess this is as good a place as any," said Velma. She steered her bike onto the mill's gravel lane. She, Fred, and Daphne parked their bikes near the entrance, noticing Shaggy and Scooby's tandem bike leaning on a nearby tree.

They walked inside through a creaky old screen door. The room was full of a variety of jars and bagged goods. Dried fruits and preserves, honey, and hard candy lined the wooden shelves. A middle-aged woman stood behind the counter that separated the customers from the kitchen. She had a scowl on her face nearly as large as her hairstyle.

"Can I help you?" she asked, seemingly annoyed.

"We're looking for our friends," Fred replied. "Their bike's outside."

"Seating's out back," said the woman. She turned away from the gang to get back to frying donuts. She seemed to respect the donuts way more than her customers.

Daphne led the way out the back door of the mill and into a grassy backyard. There were six or seven picnic tables on the grounds. Some stood in the shade of nearby trees. Others were baking in the afternoon sun.

Daphne couldn't help but be surprised by the amount of people behind the mill. Every table had a few customers seated at it. There were many more customers than the handful of cars in the parking lot.

At the closest table sat Scooby and Shaggy, both chowing down on a box of fresh apple donuts. From all appearances, they were on their second box already. A third waited patiently on the table for their attention. Daphne had no doubt that it wouldn't have to wait much longer.

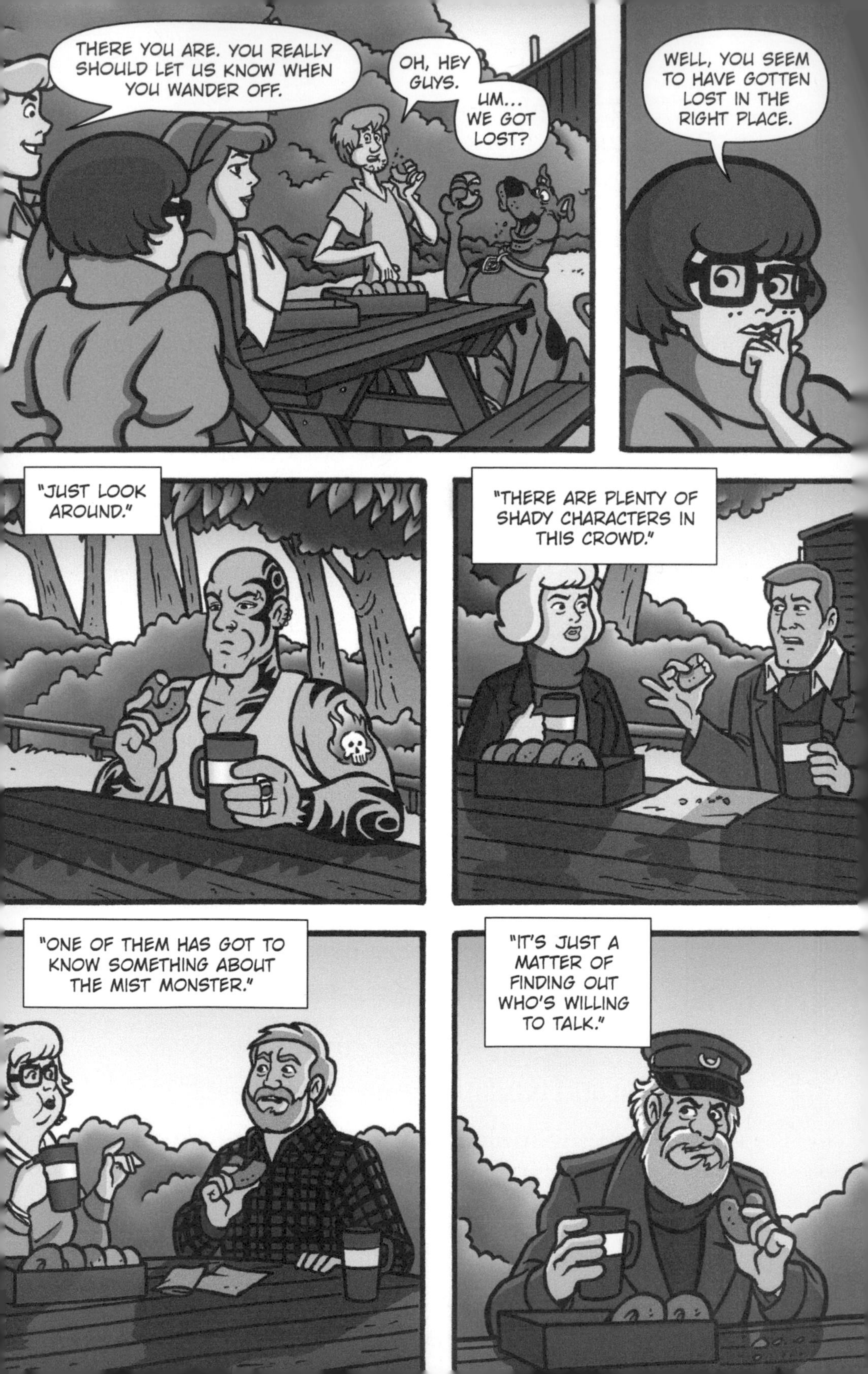
THERE YOU ARE. YOU REALLY SHOULD LET US KNOW WHEN YOU WANDER OFF.
OH, HEY GUYS.
UM... WE GOT LOST?
WELL, YOU SEEM TO HAVE GOTTEN LOST IN THE RIGHT PLACE.
"JUST LOOK AROUND."
"THERE ARE PLENTY OF SHADY CHARACTERS IN THIS CROWD."
"ONE OF THEM HAS GOT TO KNOW SOMETHING ABOUT THE MIST MONSTER."
"IT'S JUST A MATTER OF FINDING OUT WHO'S WILLING TO TALK."

MUNCH! MUNCH! MUNCH!

Scooby-Doo and Shaggy devoured dozens of donuts, one by one.

"Like, someone needs to invent a faster way to eat donuts, Scoobs," Shaggy offered.

Scooby-Doo looked around. Using his detective skills, he found a small stick on the ground. Scooby slid the stick through the holes of a dozen donuts. "Ropen rup!" he told Shaggy.

ZWIP! The donuts slid off the stick and into Shaggy's mouth.

"You're a genius, Scoobs!" Shaggy exclaimed, munching a mouthful of the tasty pastries.

As Scooby-Doo and Shaggy continued to feast on their three-course snack, Velma scanned the picnic grounds. She couldn't remember the last time she saw such a collection of suspicious characters. Velma believed that every mystery had a solution. If she was going to get to the bottom of this Mist Monster nonsense, she had to start somewhere.

"Let's go talk to some of the locals," she said. Fred and Daphne nodded, and the three headed to the next closest picnic table.

"Huh?" said Shaggy, momentarily looking up from his snack. But his friends were already gone. Shaggy shrugged and got back to the job at hand.

"Excuse me," said Velma as she approached the man at the nearest table. He had several interesting tattoos. Velma couldn't help but stare at one that looked like a flaming skull.

The young man swallowed the bite of donut he was working on, and nodded in Velma's direction.

"Sorry to bother you, but have you heard anything about a . . . well, a Mist Monster?" Velma asked. "Some creature with glowing red eyes surrounded in fog?"

The man looked at Velma for a second. He blinked, and then returned to his donut.

"Hmph!" Daphne exclaimed. "I guess that's a no, then."

The gang moved to the next table where a bored couple sat, each sipping from a cup of cider. Neither seemed to acknowledge the other.

"Hi," said Fred. "We were wondering if we could ask you a few questions."

"Ask Howard," said the woman. "He loves to talk. Sometimes he'll drone on for hours about nothing at all."

The man, who apparently was named Howard, rolled his eyes at his wife. Then he looked at Fred. "What do you need, young man?"

"We're new to town and we heard rumors about a Mist Monster?" Fred said. "Any truth to those?"

"Why, don't be absurd," said Howard. "The only monster in Mystic is the woman sitting at the table with me." Howard's wife snorted, then sipped her cider.

"See, our van went missing and then we, well, we kind of saw these two glowing eyes in a cloud of fog," Daphne said.

"Oh dear," said Howard. "That makes for a charming story. But I'm afraid we can't help you. We have no use for . . . vans, as it were."

"Friendly crowd," Velma said as the gang moved to the next table.

"I heard your story," said the old woman sitting there with her husband. "Real shame."

"One less car on the road, you ask me," interrupted her husband. "Been living in this town for fifty years and traffic's never been so bad. Why I —" One look from his wife, and the old man stopped talking. He decided to take a bite of his donut instead.

"Don't mind Jonathan," said the old woman. "And don't believe what those other people told you. Mystic's not safe anymore." Suddenly, the wind picked up, as if it were frightened by the old woman's voice. "There's something strange happening around here. If I were you, I'd keep on moving until I got to the next town."

"Suits me fine," said Jonathan as he finished his donut.

Next, the gang turned their attention to a man dressed like a grizzled old sea captain. He looked like the sort of person who'd spend his life hunting the oceans for a whale that had wronged him. But as the gang headed over to speak to him, they heard a bit of commotion near the back entrance of the cider mill.

Shaggy and Scooby-Doo were standing near the door, arguing with the woman who had been working behind the counter.

"Like, what do you mean the next batch isn't ready yet?" Shaggy said. "Do you expect us to just go hungry?!"

"Reah! Ri'm starving!" Scooby added.

"Guys, leave the poor woman alone," ordered Daphne as she and the others walked over to their friends. "Don't you think three boxes of donuts is enough?"

But Shaggy didn't hear Daphne's question. The sound of Scooby-Doo's chattering teeth drowned it out.

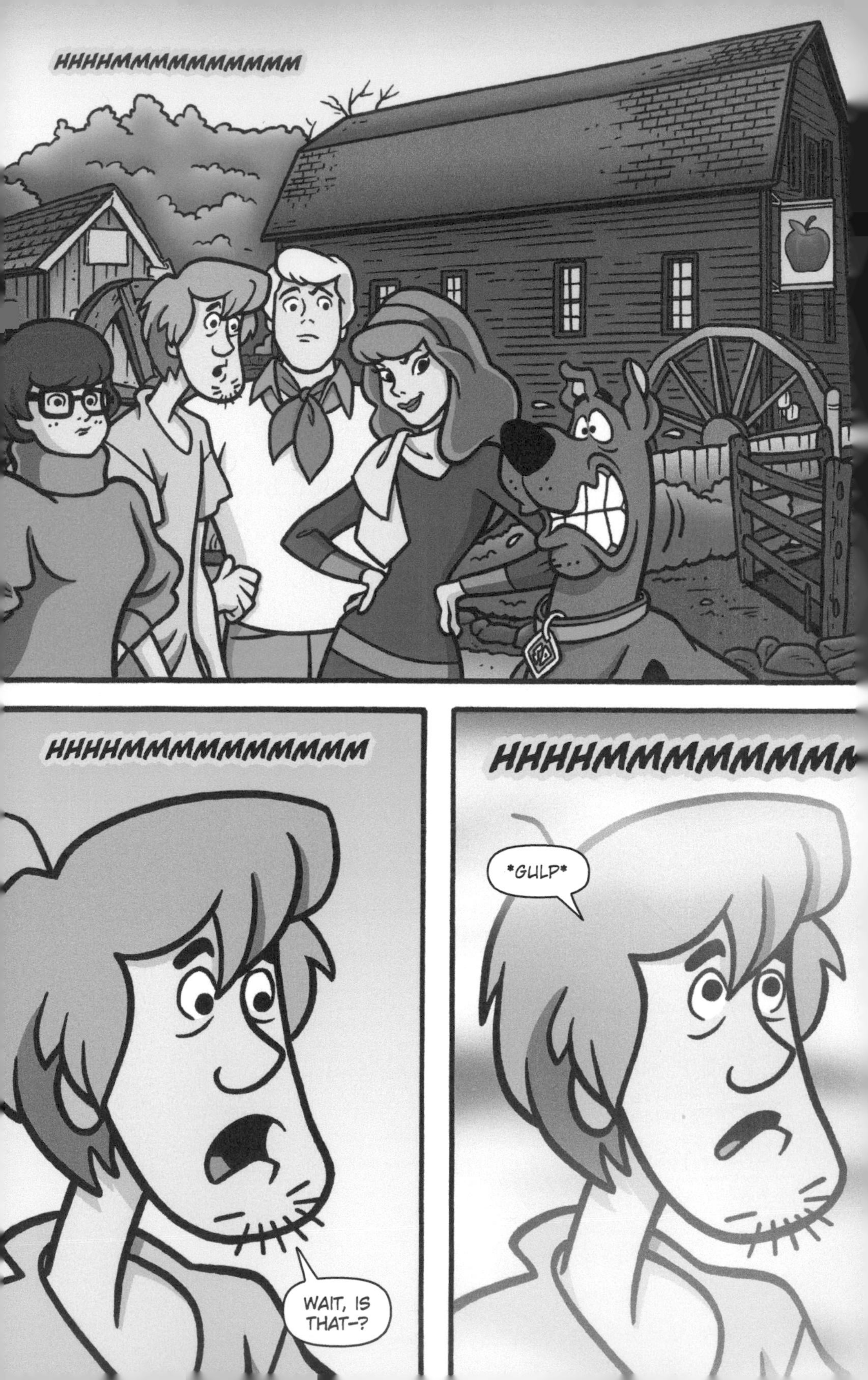
HHHHMMMMMMMMMM
HHHHMMMMMMMMMM
WAIT, IS THAT–?
HHHHMMMMMMMMM
GULP

It didn't take long for Shaggy to hear the humming noise over the sound of Scooby's teeth. And even if he hadn't heard, the mist that had suddenly surrounded the gang would probably have clued him in.

"The Mist Monster!" Shaggy exclaimed. But only Scooby was there to hear him. It seemed the crowd had disappeared from the picnic area. And more than that, Fred, Daphne, and Velma had also vanished. "Like, where did everybody go?" Shaggy asked Scooby.

Scooby didn't answer. The fog had gotten thicker now, and he could barely even see Shaggy.

The hum grew louder. So much so that Shaggy couldn't stand to stay in one place any longer.

"C'mon, Scoobs!" he shouted, as he began to feel his way toward the cider mill's back door. It was only a few feet away, but the mist was so dense that Shaggy couldn't figure out where the mill even was.

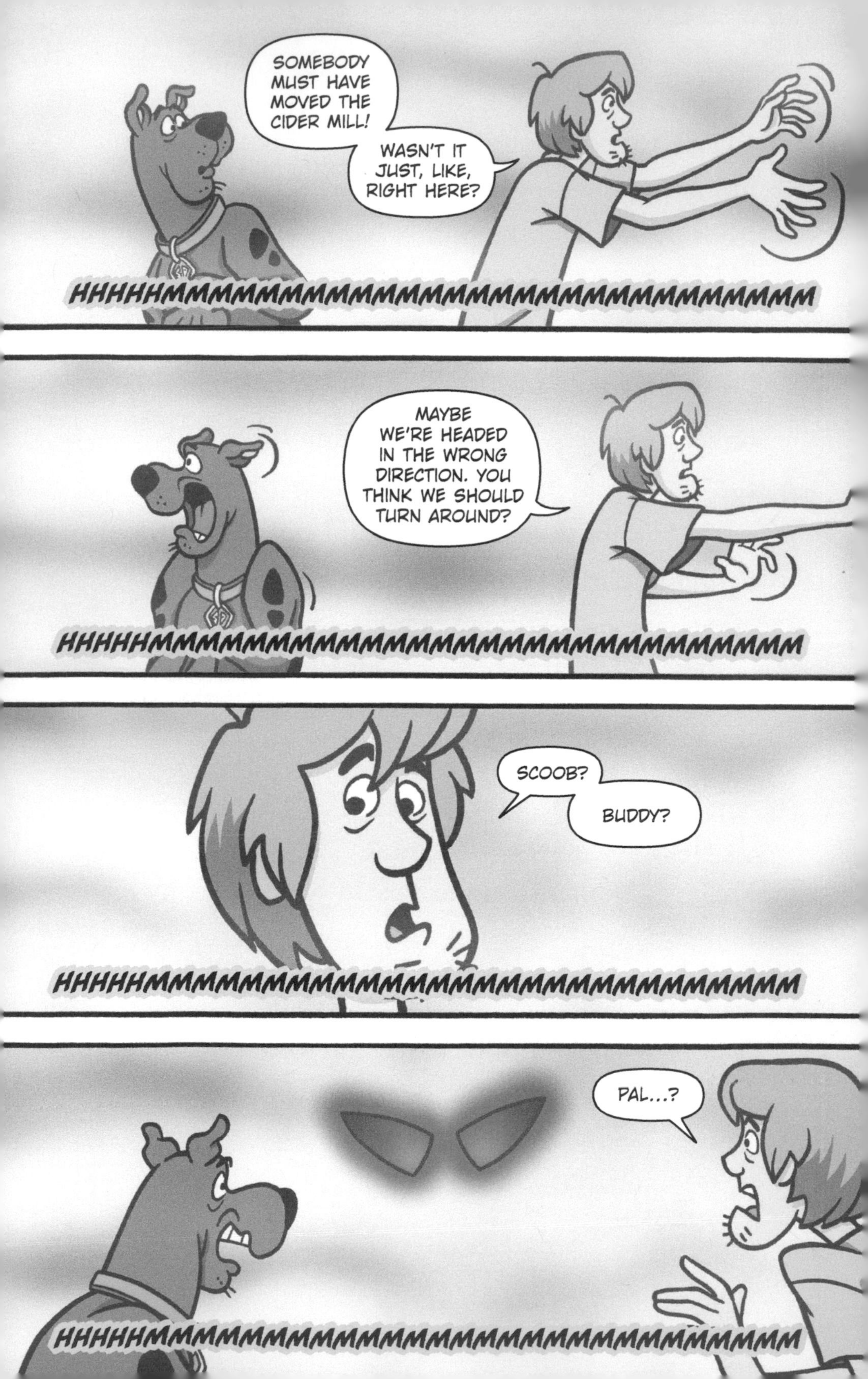
SOMEBODY MUST HAVE MOVED THE CIDER MILL!
WASN'T IT JUST, LIKE, RIGHT HERE?
HHHHHMMMMMMMMMMMMMMMMMMMMMMMMMMM
MAYBE WE'RE HEADED IN THE WRONG DIRECTION. YOU THINK WE SHOULD TURN AROUND?
HHHHHMMMMMMMMMMMMMMMMMMMMMMMMMMM
SCOOB?
BUDDY?
HHHHHMMMMMMMMMMMMMMMMMMMMMMMMMMM
PAL...?
HHHHHMMMMMMMMMMMMMMMMMMMMMMMMMMM

The Mist Monster was standing there, not a few feet away from Shaggy. It didn't move. It just stared down at him through the thick fog.

"Run!" Shaggy yelled when he could finally find the words. It was the only thing he could think to say, even though he doubted Scooby-Doo needed to hear it. In fact, Scooby was already ahead of him. He was sprinting through the fog in the opposite direction. It was all Shaggy could do to just keep up.

On any given day, the simple art of walking was a difficult enough chore for Shaggy. His feet had a way of tripping him up when he least expected it. So today, in the middle of this thick fog, he really didn't stand much of a chance.

To his credit, Shaggy made it a good dozen yards or so before his foot hit a rock that had no business being directly underneath him. He lost his balance, and before he knew it, he was rolling down a hill.

It took at least two minutes for Scooby and Shaggy to realize they were in water.

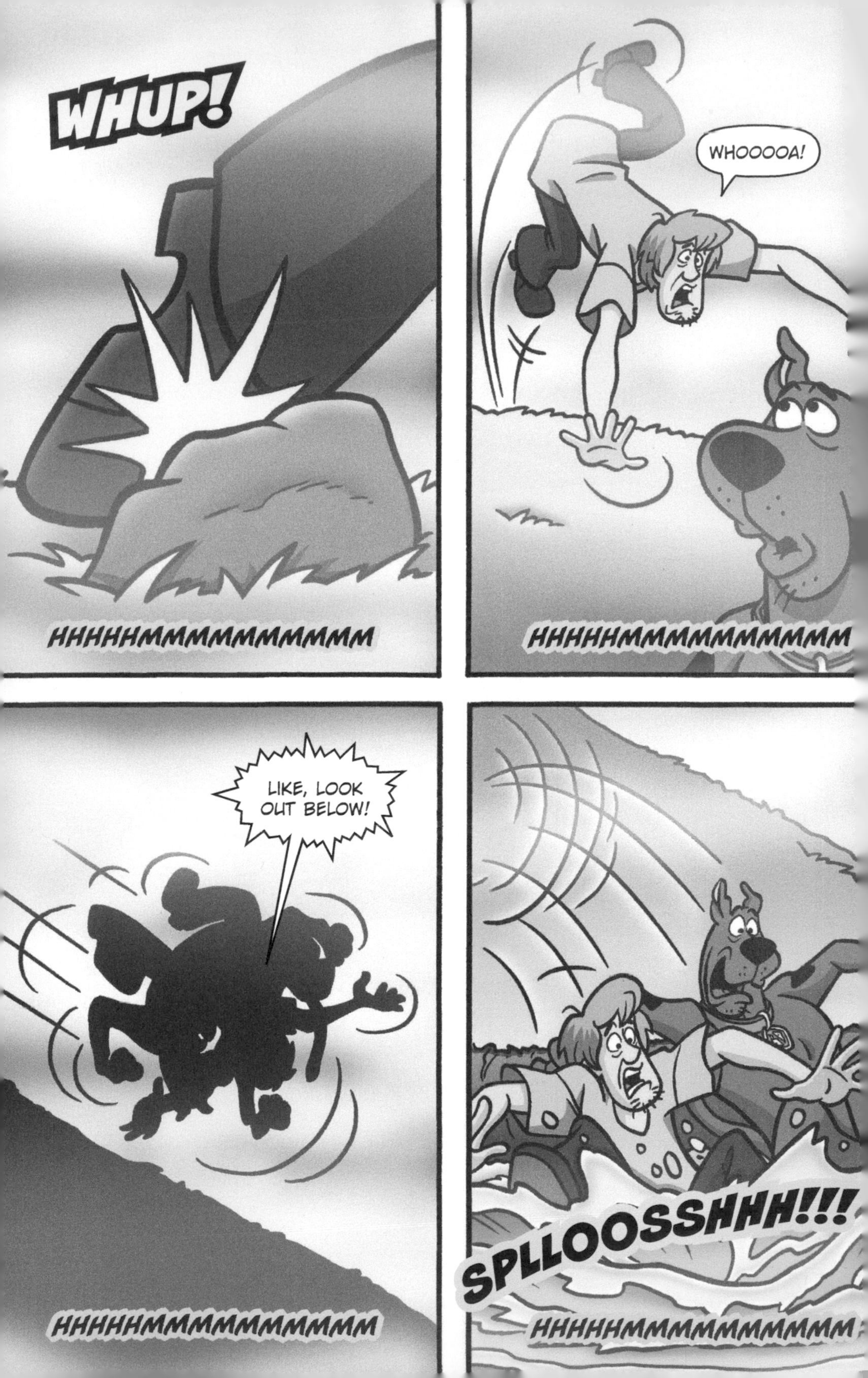
WHUP!
HHHHHMMMMMMMMMM
WHOOOOA!
HHHHHMMMMMMMMMMM
LIKE, LOOK OUT BELOW!
HHHHHMMMMMMMMMMM
SPLLOOSSHHH!!!
HHHHHMMMMMMMMMMM

It wasn't until the hum of the Mist Monster had faded away that they realized they'd rolled all the way down the hill into the small stream below.

Shaggy stood up. He did his best to ring his shirt out. It didn't help when Scooby-Doo walked over next to him and shook out his fur.

"Gee, like, thanks a million, Scoob," Shaggy said.

"Rorry," said Scooby, cringing a little.

CHAPTER 4
OUT OF THE FOG

The fog had lifted now, and the two found enough courage to head back up the hill. They walked through the picnic grounds and then into the cider mill and out its front door.

Most of the mill's customers were in the parking lot. All of them seemed really confused by what was going on. Standing in the middle of the crowd was Daphne, Fred, and Velma.

"Scooby-Doo!" Velma exclaimed when she saw them.

"Well that's a warm welcome," Shaggy said.

"And Shaggy!" Velma shouted, trying to sound as excited as before. It didn't really work.

"We were worried about you guys," said Fred. "When the fog hit, we thought you were right behind us when we ran into the mill."

"Well worry no more," said Shaggy. "We looked the Mist Monster in the eyes and told him to scram."

"Really?" asked Daphne.

"It was sort of like that," Shaggy admitted. "I mean, it's so hard to remember now. There was definitely eye-looking involved."

"Rand scramming!" Scooby added.

"Well while you guys were facing down your demons," said Fred, "Mr. and Mrs. Cooper's car was stolen."

"Who?" Shaggy said.

"Why mine, young man," said the elderly lady that the gang had spoken to earlier. "My husband's filing a police report right now."

"And we're going to do everything in our power to find that car," said Velma to Mrs. Cooper.

"Oh, don't involve yourself, dear," said the old woman. "There's something terrible happening around here. I don't want you and your friends getting hurt."

"We're no strangers to danger," Fred explained.

"Yeah, danger's like our next-door neighbor," added Shaggy. "The worst neighbor ever."

Mrs. Cooper gave Shaggy a concerned pat on the shoulder, before shuffling back into the store.

"Psst!" came a noise from behind the gang.

Fred turned around first and saw a slim figure duck behind a parked truck. Fred furrowed his brow. Then he walked toward the rust-covered pickup.

Velma and Daphne followed. As did Scooby and Shaggy as soon as they noticed they were standing in the parking lot alone.

Fred had seen the young man earlier, eating a donut at a table in the mill's backyard. He was covered in tattoos and had a few piercings on his face to complete the look he was so desperately trying for. Before Fred could say anything, the man spoke.

"You folks lost your car, right?" the man whispered.

"That's right," answered Fred. "Well, our van, I mean."

"You're not alone," said the man as he itched his skull tattoo. "I'm just passing through town, and my motorcycle was stolen when I popped into a diner for some clam chowder."

"Oh, man!" Shaggy exclaimed. "Which diner was it? We should definitely investigate that chowder."

The man seemed to ignore Shaggy. "We're not alone," he said. "People been losing all sorts of cars around here. That mist rolls in, and next thing you know, their wheels are just gone. Vanished."

"Because of the Mist Monster?" asked Velma quietly.

"That's what they been saying. They say it comes to town from up the river. Seems to like tourists' cars best."

"What would a monster want with cars?" Daphne wondered aloud.

"That's all I know," said the tattooed man. "You find my bike, you let me know, all right?"

"Will do," said Fred. The man with the skull tattoo looked both ways as if to see if anyone was watching. Then he walked away from the Mystery Inc. gang.

"Like, wait!" Shaggy called after him. "You forgot to tell us where you got the chowder!"

If the man heard Shaggy, he didn't react. He just kept on walking toward the road.

***

"Like, I think we made the right decision," said Shaggy as he and Scooby-Doo walked toward the drawbridge on Main Street.

Scooby nodded his head in agreement. The two had decided to part ways with their fellow Mystery Inc. teammates to head back to the center of town.

Daphne, Velma, and Fred were determined to head up river in search of the Mist Monster's lair. But that plan didn't sit well with Scooby and Shaggy. Shaggy thought it made the most sense to stake out the areas where they had already seen the Monster. And what better place than the Mystic drawbridge?

If that bridge just happened to neighbor an ice cream shop, then that was just good luck. It only made sense that Scooby and Shaggy had an ice-cream cone or two while they waited for the Mist Monster to rear its ugly head. After all, nobody could be expected to have a good monster hunt on an empty stomach.

"After you, old pal," said Shaggy as he held the door of the ice cream shop open for Scooby-Doo.

"Rank rou," said Scooby.

The two walked into the shop, and licked their lips. In front of them was a chalkboard with a list of way too many flavors: chocolate, vanilla, mint chocolate chip, strawberry, cookie dough, butterscotch, cookies and cream, rocky road, and more than a dozen other flavors. The air hung with the sweet smell of chocolates and waffle cones.

"Oh, man," said Shaggy. "This is going to be harder than I thought."

"Can I help you?" asked the young man behind the counter.

"I can't decide," said Shaggy. "I guess I'll just have one."

"One? One of what?" said the boy.

"Everything," Shaggy replied. "One scoop of everything."

"Rwo!" exclaimed Scooby.

"I stand corrected," said Shaggy. "Two scoops of everything."

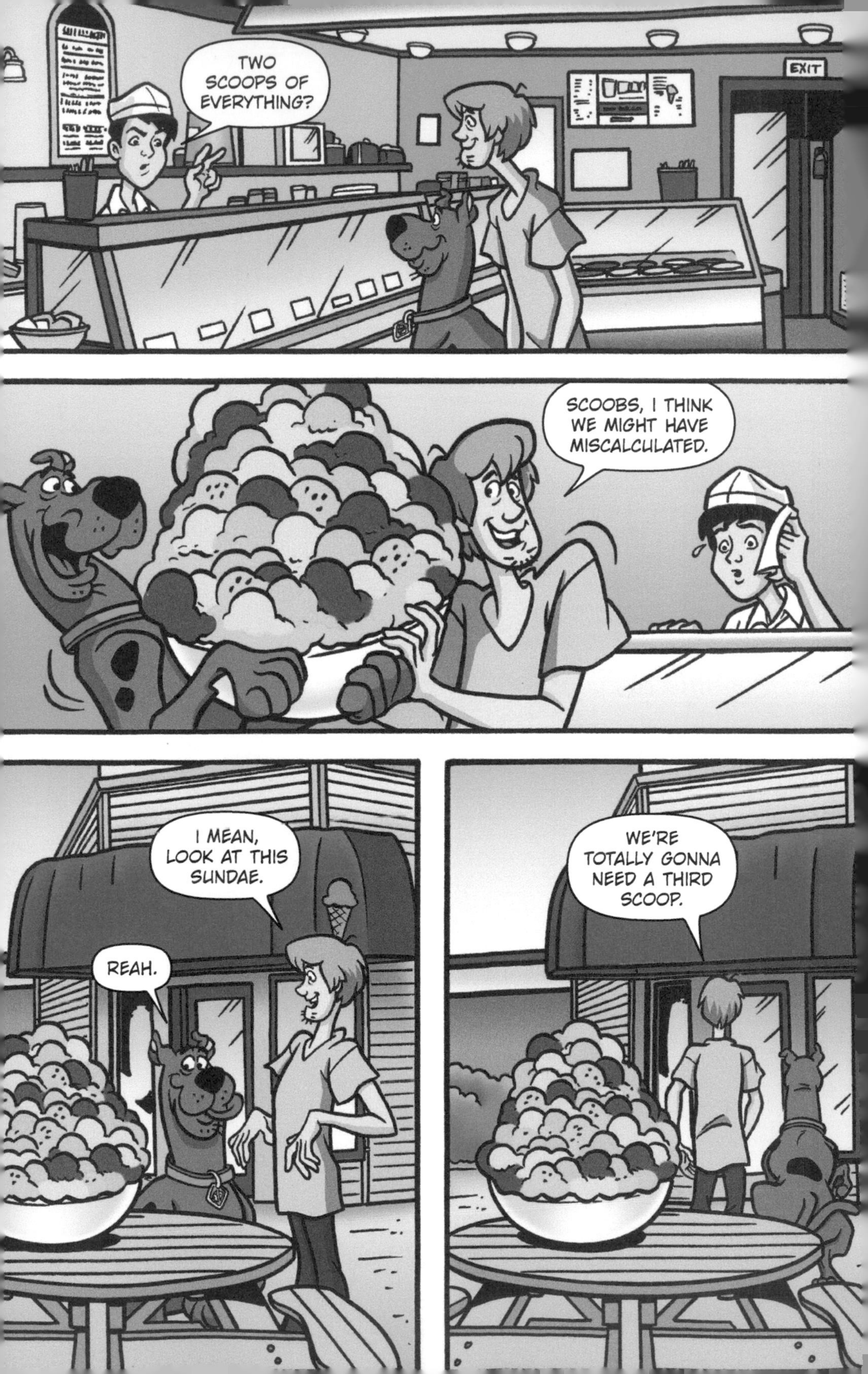
TWO SCOOPS OF EVERYTHING?
SCOOBS, I THINK WE MIGHT HAVE MISCALCULATED.
I MEAN, LOOK AT THIS SUNDAE.
REAH.
WE'RE TOTALLY GONNA NEED A THIRD SCOOP.
EXIT

A few minutes later, Scooby and Shaggy were seated in front of a mountain of ice cream. They both stared wide-eyed at the creation they'd inspired.

"It's so beautiful," said Shaggy.

"Reautiful," Scooby agreed.

They sat at a picnic table on the side of the ice cream shop. It overlooked the water of Mystic River as well as the drawbridge the two were supposed to be watching.

"Like, I don't know which flavor to try first," Shaggy said. He held his spoon in his hand as he eyed a particularly interesting scoop of chocolate in the middle of the ice cream tower.

Scooby didn't reply. He was concentrating on a mint chocolate chunk scoop on the sundae's very top. It stood a bit higher than his head, and Scooby was trying to figure out how best to reach the refreshing-looking flavor. They were both so distracted, neither Scooby-Doo nor Shaggy noticed the faint hum coming from the direction of Main Street.

HUMMMMMMMMMMMM!

"I'm going for rum raisin," said Shaggy.
"No . . . double chocolate fudge. No, strawberry
cream." Shaggy moved his spoon up and down
the sundae like a broken elevator. He couldn't
decide where to start.

HUMMMMMMMMMMMM!

The hum got louder. But Shaggy and Scooby
didn't notice.

Shaggy turned to his old friend. "This is the
hardest thing I've ever had to do," he said.
Scooby nodded in agreement.

HUMMMMMMMMMMMM!

The hum got louder still. But Shaggy and
Scooby didn't pay it any attention.

"Let's just go for it!" Shaggy raised his spoon
up and turned his head away from the dessert.
"Let fate decide!" he said.

He and Scooby-Doo raised their spoons. They
clinked them together to celebrate the first bite.

CLINK CLINK!

Then they each plunged their spoons into the gigantic sundae. Scooby-Doo pulled out a heaping spoonful of rocky road. Shaggy managed a spoonful of strawberry.

"One . . . ," Shaggy counted, holding the dripping scoop near his mouth.

"Rwo . . . ," Scooby continued to count.

"THREE!" they shouted together and then both devoured their spoonfuls.

"Rummy!" Scooby exclaimed, closing his eyes and savoring the melting ice cream on his tongue. Shaggy did the same.

When they finally opened their eyes, the sundae was gone! Well, not exactly.

Shaggy didn't plunge his spoon into pralines and cream or vanilla fudge swirl. He didn't even move an inch. Because now he could barely see Scooby-Doo sitting next to him.

The mist had rolled in.

HUMMMMMMMMMMMMM!

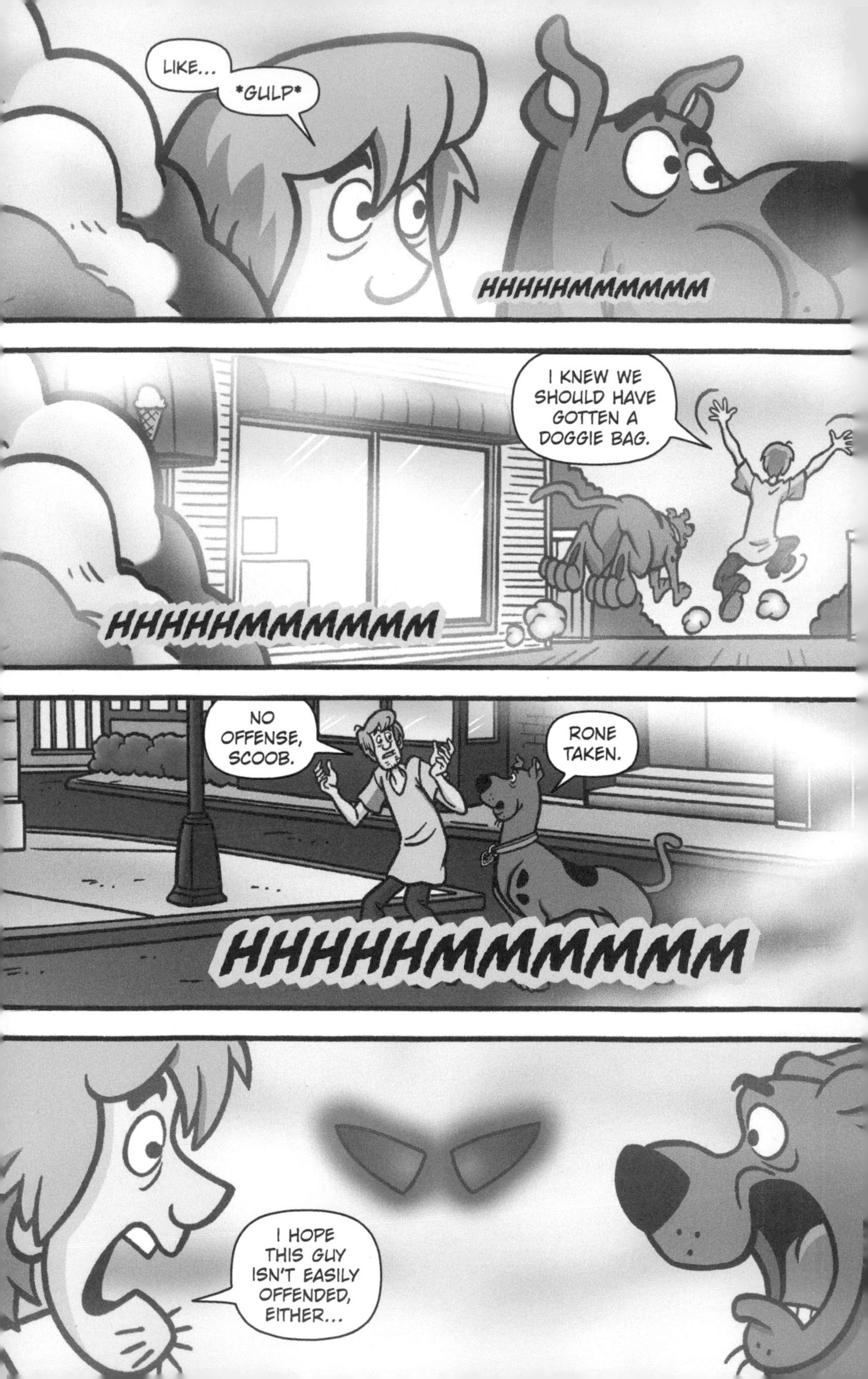
LIKE...
GULP
HHHHHMMMMMM
I KNEW WE SHOULD HAVE GOTTEN A DOGGIE BAG.
HHHHHMMMMMM
NO OFFENSE, SCOOB.
RONE TAKEN.
HHHHHMMMMMM
I HOPE THIS GUY ISN'T EASILY OFFENDED, EITHER...

HUMMMMMMMMMMM!

"Ahhhhh!" screamed Shaggy and Scooby-Doo as the Mist Monster continued chasing them or surrounding them or whatever.

"Like, which way do we go, Scoobs?" asked Shaggy, hanging onto Scooby-Doo's collar.

"Rat way!" Scooby exclaimed.

"Which way?" Shaggy asked.

"Rat way!" Scooby repeated.

"Scoobs, I can't see which way you're pointing," Shaggy said.

"Re reither!" Scooby barked.

HUMMMMMMMMMMM!

The sound grew louder. They didn't have any more time to think.

"RUN!" they both shouted.

BONK! The two friends ran directly into each other.

"The other way!" cried Shaggy as they took off in opposite directions.

Meanwhile, Fred, Daphne, and Velma had been making good time on their bikes. Shaggy and Scooby-Doo had done nothing but slow them down earlier. It was hard to get any serious biking done when two of their group were constantly distracted by the smells coming from restaurants. In fact, the gang had just now started to slow down, and it wasn't by choice. It was because they had just steered directly into another patch of thick fog.

"Okay, guys," said Fred. "Keep a look out."

"I don't see how," said Velma. She was having trouble making sure she was even on the road.

"As long as we don't see any glowing red eyes, I think we're okay," said Daphne.

Velma stopped her bike. "We've got to be at the center of it now," she said. "The mist is ridiculously thick here."

She swung her leg over her bicycle's frame and onto the ground below. But her foot didn't hit pavement. It landed on gravel.

"I think this is someone's driveway," she said. Velma always liked to be sure when she made an observation. But the fog was so dense in front of her, she didn't have that luxury at the moment.

"It's as good a lead as any," said Daphne. She hopped off her bike and gently rested it on the ground. Fred followed suit and the three began to head down the gravel lane.

After a few minutes of cautious shuffling through the mist, Daphne let out a loud, "There!"

It was hard to see exactly what she was pointing at. But with a little squinting, Fred and Velma could make out the roof of a large red barn. The gang headed for it, picking up the pace as much as they could.

A few second later, and Fred almost collided with the barn's sliding door. "Give me a hand with this," he said.

Velma and Daphne added their strength to his. The three slid the door open, revealing the barn's fog-free interior. As the mist began to seep in through the large open door, Velma's mouth fell open in surprise. There in front of her was an empty horse's stable, as well as a dozen or so parked vehicles.

Not only was the Mystery Machine among their number, but there was also a motorcycle resting in the corner. It was covered with so many skull decals, it just had to belong to the tattooed man they'd met at the cider mill.

"Jackpot!" Daphne exclaimed.

"Now we just have to find out who owns this barn," said Fred.

But Velma was already one step ahead of him. She'd wandered out of the barn and discovered a small farmhouse hiding just next to it in the fog. By the time Daphne and Fred caught up to her, she was already peering in a dark window.

"I can't see anything," said Velma. "Can you?"

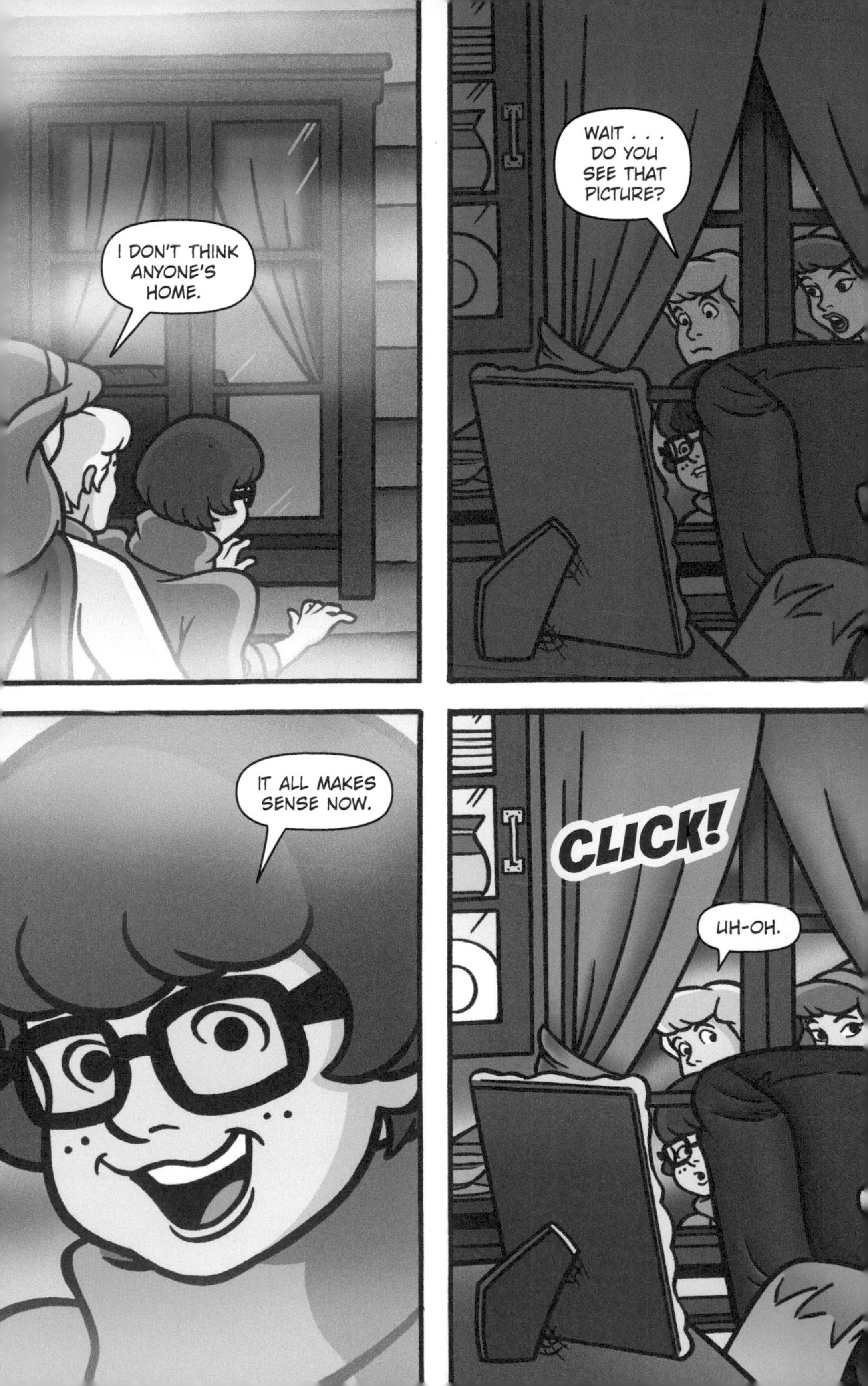
I DON'T THINK ANYONE'S HOME.
WAIT . . . DO YOU SEE THAT PICTURE?
IT ALL MAKES SENSE NOW.
CLICK!
UH-OH.

CHAPTER 5
CLEARING THINGS UP

As soon as the light had switched on inside the window, the gang knew they had no other choice. They took off running. Unfortunately, the fog didn't help them make their getaway any quicker. Before they knew it, Velma had tripped and fallen on the damp grass.

WHUMP!

"You okay?" Fred called to her, but Velma didn't answer.

"Velma?" Daphne said.

Velma and Fred stopped in their tracks. They turned and slowly retraced their steps.

"I'm fine," Velma said when they finally made their way over to her. "But I think I broke this fog machine."

CRACKLE! POP! FIZZ!

The machine sparked and flashed. Then the strange humming noise finally stopped.

She was smiling as she said it and with good reason. Another piece of the puzzle had just come together. They knew who was behind the mystery of the Mist Monster, and now Velma had a good idea how they did it.

"They must have at least a dozen of these things around the property," she said, pointing to the machine. "All this fog, it's artificial."

"That explains the humming," said Fred.

"Hey!" a voice yelled from the direction of the farmhouse. "Who's out there?"

"C'mon!" Fred said as he helped Velma to her feet.

Even though Velma had a slight limp from tripping over the machine, the three teens made it back to the barn in record time. Fred jumped behind the wheel of the Mystery Machine van. He stuck his hand in his pocket and pulled out his keys.

"Hey, you!" the voice yelled again through the fog. It seemed to be getting closer.

"You might try to hurry it up a bit," Daphne said to Fred.

Fred twisted the keys in the ignition. The Mystery Machine wouldn't start!

"I told you this van needed a tune-up!" cried Daphne as the angry man neared.

Fred twisted the key again and again until finally — **VROOOOOOM!** The Mystery Machine roared to life.

"Hey!" screamed the nearby voice.

But it was too late. The Mystery Machine was already halfway up the gravel lane.

***

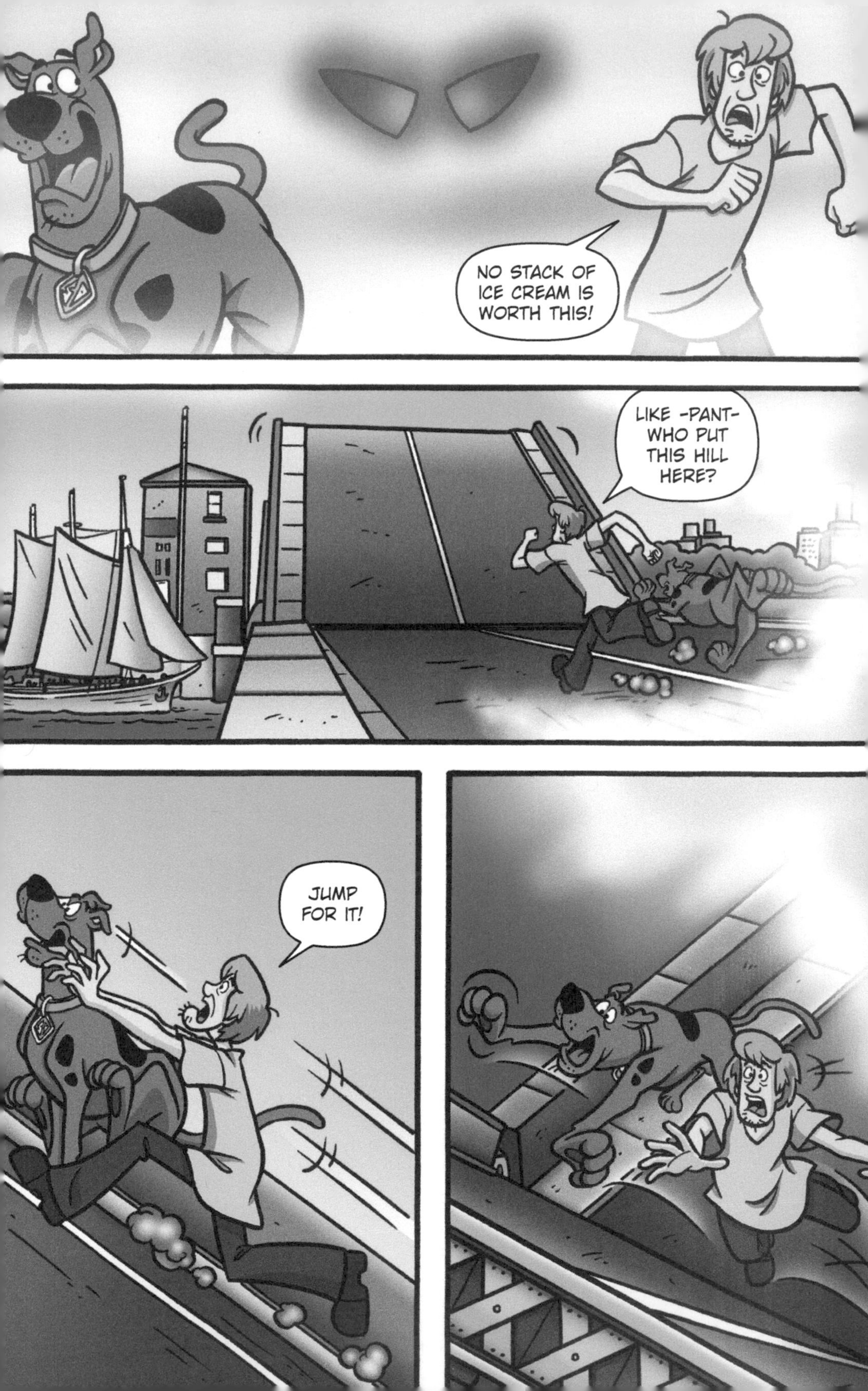
NO STACK OF ICE CREAM IS WORTH THIS!
LIKE -PANT- WHO PUT THIS HILL HERE?
JUMP FOR IT!

Shaggy hadn't been paying much attention to his surroundings ever since he'd seen the Mist Monster float slowly toward him on Main Street. If he had been paying attention, Shaggy wouldn't have run toward the drawbridge. He wouldn't have been forced to run up the slowly rising platform with the Mist Monster close behind him. And he most certainly wouldn't now be hanging for his life from the top of the open bridge alongside Scooby-Doo.

"This seemed like a good idea to me at the time," Shaggy said to Scooby.

"Re roo!" Scooby agreed.

Unfortunately, they now both realized that they'd made a horrible mistake.

Against his better instincts, Shaggy looked down. Below him was a haze of mist and fog.

HUMMMMMMMM!

In the middle of it all were the glowing red eyes of the Mist Monster gazing up at him. Shaggy noticed the pain in his fingers. It was getting harder and harder to hang on.

HUMMMMMMMMM!

"Scooby? Buddy old pal?" Shaggy said quietly to his canine friend. "Like, this might be the end of us."

"Reah, re end!" Scooby agreed, starting to whimper a little.

"There's just one thing I have to say before we let go," added Shaggy. "I really wish —" Shaggy's voice started to quiver. It sounded like he was about to cry.

"Rwhat?" Scooby pressed.

"I really wish that," Shaggy continued, "we'd have finished that sundae."

"Re too!" Scooby-Doo cried out, letting the tears spray from his eyes like sprinklers.

BEEEEEEEEEEEEP!

Just then, Shaggy heard a loud horn sounding on the water. He looked to his right as the bright white mast of a sailboat slowly made its way past.

BEEEEEEEEEEEEEP!

"Don't mind us," Shaggy said. "Take your time." He felt his fingers begin to slip a little more. A sudden gust of wind blew by, making it even harder for Shaggy to hold on.

"Rit's rindy!" said Scooby.

"I know it's windy, pal," said Shaggy. "But just hang on."

"No, rit's rindy!" Scooby-Doo shouted again. Shaggy was trying to concentrate on his grip, but he looked over at Scooby anyway. Scooby-Doo was pointing to the street below them. The wind was blowing so hard, it was beginning to clear the fog.

"Like, what is that?" Shaggy said. He squinted to get a better look.

Far below his dangling legs still loomed the two glowing eyes of the Mist Monster. But as the wind pushed the fog away, it was clear the eyes were just red lights, strung up on two thin poles. Shaggy strained to see better. The poles were attached to the saddle of a black horse that was in turn pulling a small carriage.

The carriage was hard to see, as fog continued to billow out of the machines it was hauling. But with another gust of wind, Shaggy could clearly make out a small man sitting atop the rig. It was the little old farmer from the cider mill. The man who hated traffic so much. It was Mr. Cooper.

Behind the carriage, Shaggy watched as the Mystery Machine pulled into view. It stopped a few feet away from Mr. Cooper's odd vehicle, trapping it. Fred, Velma, and Daphne jumped out of the Mystery Machine's front seat.

"It's the guys!" Shaggy said. "They've got that old guy boxed in!"

He extended one hand and waved to his friends. Not thinking, Scooby did the same. It only took another small gust of wind for Scooby-Doo and Shaggy to completely lose their grip on the bridge.

"AHHHHHH!" they screamed.

***

Fred hadn't really been thinking about Scooby-Doo or Shaggy that much. He hadn't seen them dangling from the drawbridge, or lose their grip when the Mystery Machine arrived. Fred had been focusing instead on Mr. Cooper. His main concern was keeping the elderly man from fleeing the scene while Daphne and Velma went to find a couple police officers.

To his credit, Mr. Cooper knew when he was beaten. He sat in his carriage, and even switched off the fog machines in the back. He knew there was no escaping, so he just grumbled a few words about meddling kids.

"So his plan was to scare off tourists with his Mist Monster," Daphne said to the police officer as she and Velma walked with him back toward Main Street. "He and his wife hated traffic so much, that they would haul off tourists' cars with the help of that horse-drawn carriage."

"Under the cover of a half dozen fog machines," said Velma.

The police officer scribbled a few notes in his notebook and said, "But you kids figured it out, right? Just you three?"

"Well, the three of us and . . ." Fred paused. "Hey, have you guys seen Shaggy and Scooby?"

Daphne and Velma didn't even have time to shrug before they heard a familiar voice call out from the sidewalk. "Your . . . friends . . . were hanging from the bridge for some reason," said the hotel concierge who stood outside his hotel's front door.

Apparently, he had stepped out from behind the front desk to see what all the commotion was about. Velma wondered if he was ever behind that desk at all. The concierge pointed over to the lowering drawbridge. But there was no sign of Scooby or Shaggy anywhere. There was just a sailboat that had recently passed under the bridge, and a slowly gathering crowd outside the ice cream shop.

"I don't see them any —" Fred began to say.

"There!" shouted Daphne.

Fred looked in the direction that she was pointing and saw Scooby-Doo and Shaggy safely aboard the passing sailboat.

"Like, hey guys!" said Shaggy. "You missed all the excitement!"

"These two belong to you?" said the man standing next to Shaggy. Fred instantly recognized him from the cider mill. Looks like there was a perfectly good reason he had been dressed like a sea captain.

"Scooby and I slid down the sail like a couple of bona fide pirates!" Shaggy called.

"More like fell down the sail," said the captain. "But, sure."

"We'll meet you guys over at the dock," Fred yelled back. "Glad you're okay!"

Fred looked over at Mr. Cooper as the police officer loaded him into the back of his parked cruiser. The officer mentioned something about going to Mr. Cooper's farm to round up his wife.

"Take your time," called Shaggy again from the boat. "We're in no hurry!"

Shaggy held up a bowl in his hands to show his friend. He and Scooby-Doo were eating lunch with the ship's crew. From the looks of it, clam chowder seemed to be on the menu.

Fred glanced back down Main Street and smiled. It looked like it was going to be a nice clear day.

BIOGRAPHIES

MATTHEW K. MANNING is the author of the Amazon best-selling hardcover *Batman: A Visual History.* He has also contributed to many comic books, including *Beware the Batman, Spider-Man Unlimited, Pirates of the Caribbean: Six Sea Shanties, Justice League Adventures, Looney Tunes,* and *Scooby-Doo, Where Are You?* When not writing comics themselves, Manning often authors books about comics, as well as a series of young reader books starring Superman, Batman, and the Flash. He currently resides in Asheville, North Carolina, with his wife Dorothy and their two daughters, Lillian and Gwendolyn.

SCOTT NEELY has been a professional illustrator and designer for many years. Since 1999, he's been an official Scooby-Doo and Cartoon Network artist, working on such licensed properties as *Dexter's Laboratory, Johnny Bravo, Courage the Cowardly Dog, Powerpuff Girls,* and more. He has also worked on *Pokémon, Mickey Mouse Clubhouse, My Friends Tigger & Pooh, Handy Manny, Strawberry Shortcake, Bratz,* and many other popular characters. He lives in a suburb of Philadelphia.

COMIC TERMS

caption (KAP-shuhn)—words that appear in a box; captions are often used to set the scene

gutter (GUHT-er)—the space between panels or pages

motion lines (MOH-shuhn LINES)—illustrator-created marks that help show movement in art

panel (PAN-uhl)—a single drawing that has borders around it; each panel is a separate scene on a spread

SFX (ESS-EFF-EKS)—short for sound effects; sound effects are words used to show sounds that occur in the art of a comic

splash (SPLASH)—a large illustration that often covers a full page or more

spread (SPRED)—two side-by-side pages in a comic book

word balloon (WURD BUH-loon)—a speech indicator that includes a character's dialogue or thoughts; a word balloon's tail leads to the speaking character's mouth

GLOSSARY

aroma (UH-roh-mah)—a noticeable and usually pleasant smell

concierge (kahn-SI-urj)—an employee at a hotel whose job is to provide help and information to the people staying at the hotel

condo (KAHN-doh)—a room or set of rooms that is owned by the people who live there and that is part of a larger building containing other similar sets of rooms

devoured (di-VOU-urd)—ate something quickly

drawbridge (DRAW-bridj)—a bridge that can be raised up so that people cannot cross it or so that boats can pass under it

mill (MIL)—a building with machines for turning grain, produce, or other materials into products

observation (ob-zur-VAY-shuhn)—something that you have noticed by watching carefully

VISUAL QUESTIONS

1. What is happening in this panel from page 44? Explain how you came to that conclusion.

2. Illustrators use motion lines to show action in art. Explain what type of action is happening in this panel from page 68? How do you know?

3. Write down all the differences in these panels from page 40. How do those differences help tell the story?

SCREEEEEEEEECCCCHHHHHH!!!!!!!

4. Sound effects, also known as SFX, make comic books come to life. Write down every SFX in this book for your own SFX dictionary!

SCOOBY-DOO JOKES!

Why are frogs always so happy?
They eat whatever bugs them!

Where did the spaghetti go to dance?
The meat ball!

What's a math teacher's favorite dessert?
Pi.

How does the Mystery gang make cookies?
With Scooby-dough!

FIND MORE SCOOBY-DOO JOKES IN...

ALSO FROM CAPSTONE!

DISCOVER MORE SCOOBY-DOO COMIC CHAPTER BOOKS!

"There's got to be dozens of holes like this," said Velma, looking down at Fred. "Strewn around this side of the mountain."

"I'm just hoppy it wasn't that deep," said Fred as he finished pushing himself back onto the surface. He hadn't fallen far. The hole he'd discovered in the ground was barely taller than him. With the help of a nearby root and a good jump, Fred had no problem boosting himself right back out again.

"So now can we go?" said Shaggy. "We found another way in. That was the goal, right?"

"But this is obviously not the entrance our 'ghosts' are using," said Fred. "It was completely covered up. You could probably get to the rest of the cave system from there, but no one has used that way for years . . . if ever."

"They're ghosts," said Shaggy. "Since when did ghosts need an entrance, anyway?"

"These do," said Daphne. She was hurrying down the hill toward her friends. "You guys may want to see this."

87

". . . I was looking through the papers on Belastic's desk, I saw a delivery note about a dozen cupcakes to be delivered to his dressing room," explained Velma. "I knew that any place with cupcakes was the most likely place to find you!"

Shaggy flushed. "Like, this was definitely the first place we looked," he said. "And we certainly only ate real food today. Right, Scoob?"

CHOMP! CHOMP! CHOMP!

Scooby wiped frosting from his mouth. "Reah," he agreed. "Ro rakeup?"

"What did he say?" asked Daphne.

"Never mind," said Shaggy, embarrassed.

94

"Did someone say jewel?" Professor Dinkley exclaimed from the other side of the dig site.

Shaggy pulled the object out of the ground and held it up in the sunlight. He cleaned off the clinging soil. Everyone gasped in surprise.

"It's a ruby!" the professor exclaimed.

"It certainly looks like one," Velma said.

"Do you know what this means, kids?" Dinkley asked excitedly.

"Yeah! Treasure!" Shaggy proclaimed.

"This discovery makes the dig site more important than ever," Professor Dinkley said.

"It also makes it a lot more valuable," Velma observed.

"Maybe the Gator Man is trying to protect the treasure," Shaggy said.

"Or trying to scare people away from it," Daphne replied.

Meanwhile, Fred studied the palm trees growing at the edge of the dig site. He had an idea of how to use them to trap the Gator Man.

88

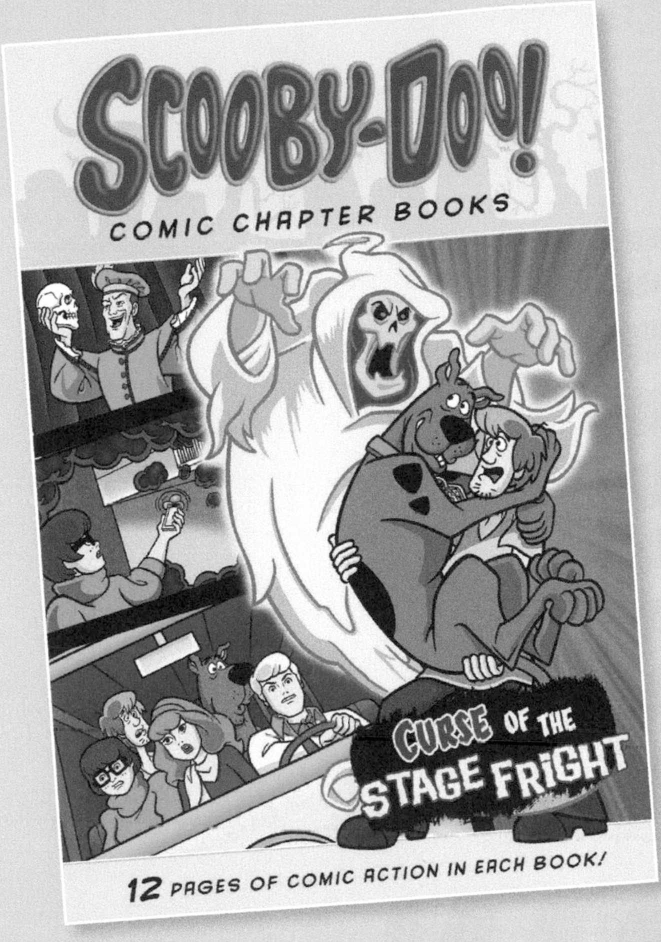
SCOOBY-DOO!
COMIC CHAPTER BOOKS
CURSE OF THE STAGE FRIGHT
12 PAGES OF COMIC ACTION IN EACH BOOK!

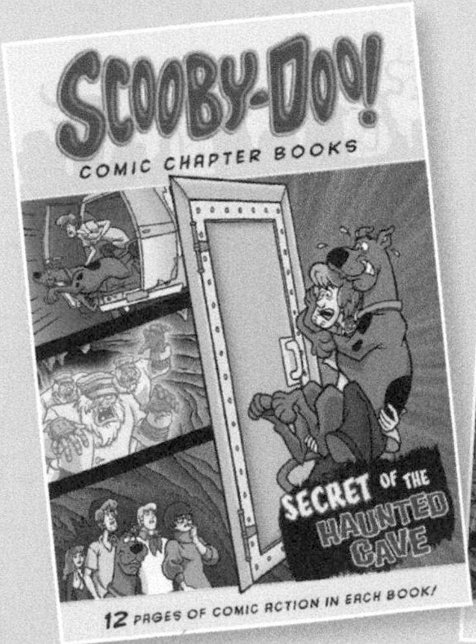
SCOOBY-DOO!
COMIC CHAPTER BOOKS
SECRET OF THE HAUNTED CAVE
12 PAGES OF COMIC ACTION IN EACH BOOK!

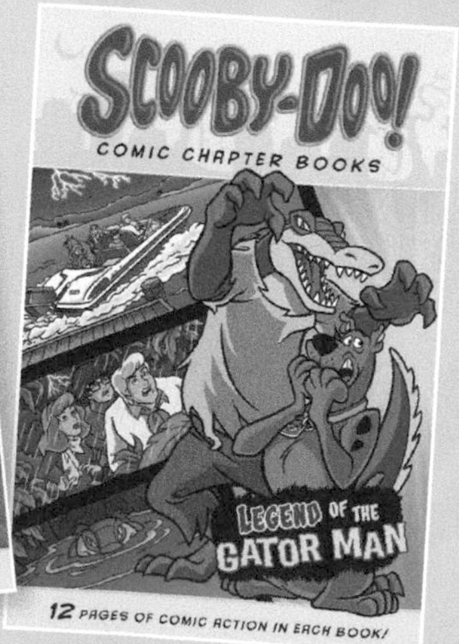
SCOOBY-DOO!
COMIC CHAPTER BOOKS
LEGEND OF THE GATOR MAN
12 PAGES OF COMIC ACTION IN EACH BOOK!

Discover more at
WWW.CAPSTONEKIDS.COM

Find cool websites and more
books like this one at

WWW.FACTHOUND.COM

Just type in the
BOOK ID: **9781496535863**
and you're ready to go!